TIME-LIFE
Early Learning Program

The
Bumbletown
Detectives

ALEXANDRIA, VIRGINIA

Note to Parents

In *The Bumbletown Detectives,* your child will join three clever sleuths in solving a variety of cases that foster critical-thinking skills. These include sorting, sequencing, and deductive reasoning, techniques that form the foundation for early learning in both mathematics and science.

When presented with a mystery, each detective describes the steps necessary to solve the problem. Then, before giving the solution, the sleuth challenges your child to guess the answer himself. After solving the first case, each detective tackles one or two additional puzzles that require similar thinking skills but are slightly more complex.

As you read the book together, encourage your child not only to guess the solution to each problem, but also to explain how he came up with it. Praise his efforts whether or not the answer is correct, emphasizing that the right approach is often more important than the right answer. If your child's answer *is* incorrect, work through the problem again, step by step, to show how to solve it correctly.

Chapter 1: The Deeds of Sneed

At Mystery Manor in the village of Bumbletown
in the land of Flugelberry, queer things were afoot.

"I'm thoroughly mystified," said Dame Edith to her husband, Sir Reginald. "Cook just told me that a dozen of your favorite raisin buns have disappeared from the pantry!"

"How very odd indeed!" replied Sir Reginald. "Last night I lost my slippers, and this morning they turned up floating in the bathtub. And whenever I plant new roses in the garden, I dig up soup bones missing from the kitchen!"

"This calls for a detective!" Dame Edith exclaimed, and the word went out that Mystery Manor needed a sleuth.

Early the next morning, Dame Edith answered a sharp knock on the door to find a dapper man singing a song:

"Here I stand in my bowler hat,
Testing out your 'Welcome' mat!"

Dame Edith read Basil's card, then his hat. Finally, she asked for proof that he was the world's greatest detective.
Replied Basil: "My latest caper is described in this paper."
And he pulled a story out of his hat:

Inside the mansion's great hall, Basil settled himself in Sir Reginald's favorite armchair. He absent-mindedly scratched the head of Butler, the couple's pet bifflebarker, who had the run of the house. Sir Reginald sat down on a footstool, while Dame Edith perched on a wing chair. Then Basil told this story:

I was making my way through the land of Ze-Ay when I got a call from Veggie Hall. Prince Carrot-top, it seems, had dashed his mother's dreams by saying he'd eat no more greens. But Queen Clara Phyll loved him still: "He's joined the circus," she told me. "If you can find him, I'll never make him eat spinach again!" Said I: "Fear not, Madam! Sneed is up and at 'em! Your tyke—what does he look like?"

Three things make my son one of a kind. Can you see what they are?

His feet are not petite. His size could win a prize. And the color of his hair is marvelously rare.

I caught up with the circus in the village of McMurkus.
Without a single stop, I headed straight for the Big Top.
What I saw inside made me want to run and hide: At least
a dozen clowns were cavorting all around. How was I to spot
young Prince Carrot-top?

Using the first of my clues, I searched for shoes as big as
You-Know-Who's.

Then what did I do? Why, I went to clue two: Only two of these three were as tall as Prince C.

When I remembered clue three, the prince was plain to see. And so the answer had been found—can *you* spy the princely clown?

Prince Carrot-top was easy to spot. The hair on his head was a bright, shining red."

Dame Edith was delighted. "Bravo for the brainwork!" she cried. "But will it be enough to solve the manor's mysterious events? I'd like you to take a test of my own."

"Indeed? Proceed!"

Dame Edith summoned her three children, who happened to be triplets. As they skipped into the great hall, she said, "Basil T. Sneed, I'd like you to meet Noisy, Bob, and Hungry—but not necessarily in that order! And there lies your challenge: Which child goes by which name?"

Basil took one look at the trio and declared, "What cute little elves! They've got their names all over themselves!"

Study each kid for a clue and you can name them, too!

WORLD'S GREATEST DETECTIVE

"Hungry is the one who had fruit in his boot.

"Noisy is he with bells on his sleeves.

"Having named the first two, I know Bob must be you!"

WORLD'S GREATEST DETECTIVE

Dame Edith, Sir Reginald, and the triplets all applauded.

"That was sharp-eyed deduction, indeed!" Dame Edith told Basil. "You are just the person to find out what happened to our raisin buns, slippers, and soup bones."

No sooner had Dame Edith said these words, however, than the front door shuddered loudly. It sounded almost as if someone was kicking it.

"Just a minute, sir," Dame Edith told the figure outside, "and I will speak to your other half."

Chapter 2: How Good Is Osgood?

"Good day, sir!" Dame Edith called through the lower half of the door. "May I ask why your head is where your feet should be?"

"I have walked all night to get here," replied the upside-down man. "And now I am resting my feet."

"That's what I call using your head!" Dame Edith exclaimed. "What brings you here?"

"Why, my feet, of course!"

"No, no, no—I mean, why have you come here?"

"Well, I heard that you needed a detective. And since I, Osgood P. Pettibone, am the world's greatest detective, I rushed right over."

"How thoughtful of you," said Dame Edith. "But I was just about to hire this other detective."

"She was indeed," Basil piped up. "Or my name's not Basil T. Sneed! So go home, Pettibone!"

"But surely you would not send the great Osgood away without a test!" Pettibone objected.

"Very well," replied Dame Edith. "Come into the garden and we will see if you are truly the world's greatest."

"Your challenge," Dame Edith told Osgood, "is to find something that is in the garden. I'll give you three clues: One, it is something you eat; two, it is next to a fence; and three, it is colored red."

"That might stump an ordinary detective," said Osgood, "but for me the answer is clear! I see five things to eat...

...five things next to a fence...

...and five things that are colored red. But only one of them fits all three clues."

Do you see it, too?

"It's the tomato!" Osgood triumphantly sang out.

Dame Edith clapped her hands in delight, but Basil T. Sneed looked unhappy. "That test was so easy it made me queasy!" he blurted out. "May I ask for a task that will strain his brain?"

"All right," Dame Edith agreed. "Osgood, would you be so kind as to follow me into the greenhouse?"

As soon as Dame Edith and Osgood entered the greenhouse, she turned to the detective and said:

This time I would like you to find something that has a handle, holds water, and is not yellow.

"Hmm, that's a little tougher," said Osgood, studying all the objects in the greenhouse. "I'll start by finding everything that has a handle.

"Next, I'll pick out every one of these things that holds water.

"And finally, I'll zero in on the one object among them that is not yellow."

Can you spot it, too?

"It's the red watering can!" Osgood proudly announced.

"Goodness!" cried Dame Edith. "How did you solve my test so fast?"

"A little brainpower, Madam!" said Osgood. "And a lot of practice; just last week, you see, I cracked a similar case on the Island of Wishes. You have been there, perhaps?"

"No, I haven't," Dame Edith replied, "but it just so happens that I love a good mystery, so I would love to hear the tale."

"Very well," said Osgood, and he told this story:

The Island of Wishes is a magical place where everything you wish for comes true. I was called there by Arnold Dimpleby, who ruled the island with his twin brother, Ernest Dimpleby.

Someone has taken my Wishful Thinking Cap! Without it, I can't make wishes come true! Can you figure out where it is?

Do you have any idea who took it?

Then Arnold opened the envelope and showed me the note inside:

Go to Coconut Cove and look for something that has a shell and a flag, and is made of sand!

Whoever had taken Arnold's wishing cap was a master riddler! Only a very clever thinker, I knew, could solve this mystery. I therefore set out for Coconut Cove at once.

I looked at everything on the beach. Finally I found the one thing that had a shell and a flag, and was made of sand.

Can you spot it, too?

It was a magnificent sandcastle built upon the beach! On the back of its flag I found a note:

Next, seek something spotted. It must also have a tail and fly through the sky.

Now *this* was a brain boggler! As usual, though, Osgood P. Pettibone was equal to the task. I searched high and low until—sure enough!—I found the answer to the riddle.

Can you find it with me?

It was a spotted kite with a long tail!
I reeled in the kite to discover a
map on one side:

How to use this map:
Step 1: Find the green arrow.
Step 2: Follow the path from the green arrow to the plant that has three red flowers, and turn.
Step 3: Cross the brook on the bridge made of wood, then head straight for the wishing well. There you will find your cap!

Night was coming on and it was getting cold when at last I found Arnold's Wishful Thinking Cap. As I started back toward Dimpleby Castle, it began to rain. My detective hat got soaked. Arnold's cap looked nice and dry, so I slipped it on my head. Oh, how I wished that I was safely back in Dimpleby Castle, drinking hot chocolate with marshmallows!

The very next moment, I found myself standing right next to Arnold in Dimpleby Castle. In my hand was a cup of hot chocolate, and in the cup were several fluffy marshmallows—the Wishful Thinking Cap had granted me my wish!

"You found my precious hat!" Arnold cried out. "You must be the greatest detective the world has ever known!"

Then Arnold settled the hat on his own head and said to me, "I wish you just as much success in your next case!"

Dame Edith was visibly impressed by Osgood's tale.
"That was slick sleuthing indeed!" she congratulated
him. "But now I can't decide whether to hire you or Mr.
Sneed. Perhaps I should—"

A cry from upstairs stopped Dame Edith in mid-
sentence: "Oh, NO!" someone shouted. "Not *AGAIN!*"

They all rushed upstairs to find Sir Reginald in a soggy mood.

"That's the seventh time this week I've found my slippers in the bathtub!" Sir Reginald sputtered. "Can't *anyone* figure out what's going on in Mystery Manor?!"

Just then, a huge balloon floated by outside.

"What in the world is that?!?" they all shouted.

Chapter 3: Penelope Potts Pops In

Dame Edith, Basil, Osgood, Butler the bifflebarker, and a sopping-wet Sir Reginald ran into the courtyard, where a hot-air balloon was about to touch down.

"Greetings, group!" called the pilot. "I am Penelope Potts, the dandiest detective in all Flugelberry!"

Basil and Osgood raised their eyebrows.

Dame Edith whispered to Sir Reginald, "If there's one thing we don't need right now, it's another detective!"

"I trust I'm not too tardy," said Penelope Potts. "I was detained by some detection in New Delhi. A lad had lost his leopard, you see, and—"

Dame Edith interrupted as politely as she could. "I'm terribly sorry, Penelope, but Basil and Osgood got here long before you. I will probably choose one of them."

"Great gumshoes!" said Penelope. "They must have bagged the raisin-bun robber I've heard so much about!"

"Not quite," Dame Edith replied. "Nor do we have any idea who took the slippers or buried the soup bones."

"Then give me a chance to catch the clever crook!" Penelope pleaded.

"Very well," said Dame Edith. "But since Basil and Osgood both took a test, you will have to take one too. After that, we will pick the best detective."

Dame Edith and Sir Reginald led the Bumbletown detectives into the loom room.

"I am knitting this scarf for Sir Reginald," Dame Edith told Penelope. "Can you tell me what the next color will be?"

"That's a puzzler!" Penelope exclaimed. "But I perceive a pattern: Orange, white, green; orange, white, green. If that order stays the same, I know what color you'll knit next."

Can you name the next color too?

"I am proud to proclaim that orange is next in order," Penelope announced.

Dame Edith's face lit up, but Basil and Osgood were not so thrilled.

"That wasn't tough enough!" said Basil.

"Finding a tomato was *much* harder!" said Osgood.

Sir Reginald cleared his throat and said, "I wonder if I might give Penelope a test of my own?"

"Gladly!" said Penelope. "Please go ahead!"

Sir Reginald walked over to an enormous loom.

"I am weaving a new bath mat," he told Penelope, "because my old one is getting dog-eared. Your challenge is to guess what I will add next."

"Let's see," said Penelope. "You began the bath mat with a row of four flugelhorns. Next you added five Ferris wheels, then six sea horses. Aha! Then you started to repeat the pattern!"

Can you guess what Sir Reginald will weave next?

"It will be a row of six sea horses!" Penelope stated.

"That was fast figuring!" Sir Reginald said in awe.

"I must confess," said Basil, "I am impressed!"

"And I admire a detective who can think on her feet," admitted Osgood.

"Practice makes perfect, gentlemen," Penelope explained. "My most dazzling detection involved precisely this sort of problem! Let me tell you all about it!"

I was wafting my way to a case in Cancun when I spotted some signs in the jungle below.

That old soft shoe

Is hard to beat;

Come see our revue—

It's a special treat!

Beyond the last sign stood a theater packed with people. This was too tantalizing to pass by! I brought the balloon to earth and headed for the hubbub.

No sooner had I settled in my seat than a curious creature poked his head through the curtain.

"Is there a detective in the house?" he called out.

"Indeed there is!" I responded.

"Please come backstage!" begged the bug. Then he ducked behind the drapes.

Backstage, I found the bug waiting for me outside his dressing room.

"I need your help!" he said. "I can't figure out how to put on my costume, and the show starts in 10 minutes!"

"But your suit seems simply smashing!" I informed the insect.

"You don't know the half of it!" he replied. "Step inside and I'll show you the rest of the problem!"

"You're a many-bodied bug!" I replied.

"*Too* many," said Cucaracha. "That's why my wardrobe assistant quit! As you can see, I need a hat for each head, gloves for each pair of hands, and shoes for each pair of feet. Can you figure out which clothes go where?"

After studying Cucaracha's clothing, I saw that he was wearing only three types of outfits.

Then I realized that those outfits followed a pattern.

It took some fleet footwork, but I managed to clothe Cucaracha in his costumes in time for his opening act.

Cucaracha was the star of the show! He sang, danced, and played nine different instruments all at the same time, and not a cap or cummerbund was out of place!

Afterward, as Cucaracha waved a fond farewell, he called out to me, "You're the world's greatest detective!"
I had to admit it: Cucaracha was correct!

Chapter 4: A Triple Test

"You have a marvelous mind!" Dame Edith told Penelope Potts. "But so do Basil and Osgood! And since three people cannot be the world's greatest detective, how can I decide which one of you to hire?"

"I know how!" Sir Reginald piped up. "This way to the drawing room, everybody!"

Sir Reginald pulled a statue on the mantel toward him, and the back of the fireplace swung open.

Behind the fireplace was a secret route to the drawing room!

Sir Reginald hurried off and was soon out of sight. The others struggled to keep up by following the pointers.

Can you follow Reggie's route to the drawing room?

Finally they reached the drawing room.
"I have one last set of challenges for all three detectives," Sir Reginald announced.

Sir Reginald turned to Basil and said, "You were the first detective to reach Mystery Manor, so the first test is for you."

Then he held out three numbers.

"These numbers have fallen off the objects along this wall. Can you detect where they belong?"

Basil looked first at the numbers in Sir Reginald's hand, then at all the objects arrayed along the wall.

Can you help Basil put the numbers back where they belong?

"The '3' came unhooked from the cover of that book," said Basil.

Goldilocks and the 3 Bears

"The '2' was knocked off the face of that clock," Basil continued.

"So the '1' must have worn off that uniform! My process of elimination calls for a celebration!"

WORLD'S GREATEST DETECTIVE

Everyone toasted the process of elimination with goblets of pink grapefruit juice from the drawing-room fountain.

Next Sir Reginald turned to Osgood: "You arrived second, so the second test is for you."

Sir Reginald held up a fistful of digits. "These numbers have fallen off my telephone, my calendar, and my recipe for oatmeal cookies. Can you tell where they go?"

How do you think Osgood will sort out the jumbled numbers?

"I can see that the '8' belongs on the phone," said Osgood.

"And the '27' has fallen off your calendar.

"The '10' must therefore go on the recipe! Let's get those cookies baking!"

"Looks like riddles don't last long in Mystery Manor!" Penelope Potts exclaimed.

"I'm beginning to think you're right!" said Sir Reginald. "Let's see how you do on my third test."

Come to a banquet at Mystery Manor! Everyone in this room will be present. There will be ___ people and ___ bifflebarker. We will dine at ___ o'clock.

"I was about to invite some of my favorite detectives to dinner," Sir Reginald explained, "when the numbers on the invitations fell off. Can you put them back?"

"That's quite a quandary!" cried Penelope. "But you can count on me. Hmm…*counting*—could that be a clue?"

Penelope looked at Sir Reginald's invitation. Then she counted everyone—and every pet—in the drawing room.

"I've got it!" she gloated. "There are five people in this parlor, so the number '5' comes first. I behold but a single bifflebarker—therefore, the number '1' is next. And from this I surmise that we will sup at 6 o'clock!"

Chapter 5: The Culprit Is Collared

"Gracious!" said Dame Edith. "Not one detective was stumped by our tests!"

"Then why not hire all three?" Sir Reginald suggested.

"A splendid idea!" Dame Edith agreed.

She turned to the Bumbletown detectives. "Bring us the raisin-bun robber, the slipper nipper, and the soup-bone burglar, and we'll reward you with a feast!"

Basil, Osgood, and Penelope were eager to meet Dame Edith's challenge; the day's detecting had given everyone a big appetite.

"Let's put our heads together," said Osgood. "That might help us solve the mystery faster!"

It looks like the Bumbletown detectives are about to solve the mystery! Can you solve it too? Here are three places you might want to look for clues: near the chair shaped like a hand in the great hall; in the garden; and in the loom room.

"That was terrific teamwork!" Sir Reginald exclaimed. "I can't believe our very own bifflebarker is the culprit! How did you figure it out?"

"Sitting in your hall when I first came to call," said Basil, "I thought that your house was lived in by a mouse. Crumbs were near my chair; crumbs were everywhere! I knew the thief liked raisin buns, so I followed up that trail of crumbs. Much to my relief, they led me to the thief."

Then Osgood explained how he had cracked the case.

"I had heard that your thief was burying stolen soup bones in the garden. When you gave me the tomato test, I spotted a bone next to the hole that Butler was digging. I therefore deduced that your bifflebarker was the guilty one!"

Finally, it was Penelope's turn.

"When we were in the loom room," she revealed, "I saw Butler running away, then noticed that my goggles were gone. When Butler came back, he was soaking wet! So when my goggles turned up in my goblet, I concluded that Butler had flung them into the fountain— and that he had stolen Sir Reginald's slippers, too!"

"Hurrah for the world's greatest detectives!" Dame Edith and Sir Reginald cried out together.

Just then, the grandmother clock in the dining room chimed six bells. Sir Reginald, Dame Edith, and the Bumbletown detectives sat down to a banquet that included Dame Edith's Soup Surprise, raisin buns, pink grapefruit juice, and Reggie's World-Famous Oatmeal Cookies.

Dame Edith seated Butler at the head of the table.

"But that's the place of honor!" Sir Reginald objected. "No troublemaking bifflebarker belongs there!"

"Yes he does," Dame Edith explained. "If Butler sits where we can all keep a close eye on him, the strange doings in Mystery Manor should cease forevermore!"

Butler the bifflebarker has hidden himself all through Mystery Manor! How many places can you find him?

TIME-LIFE for CHILDREN™

Publisher: Robert H. Smith
Managing Editor: Neil Kagan
Editorial Directors: Jean Burke Crawford,
 Patricia Daniels, Allan Fallow, Karin Kinney, Sara Mark
Editorial Coordinator: Elizabeth Ward
Product Managers: Cassandra Ford, Margaret Mooney
Assistant Product Manager: Shelley L. Schimkus
Production Manager: Prudence G. Harris
Administrative Assistant: Rebecca C. Christoffersen
Special Contributor: Jacqueline A. Ball

Produced by Joshua Morris Publishing, Inc.
Wilton, Connecticut 06897.
Series Director: Michael J. Morris
Creative Director: William N. Derraugh
Illustrator: Yvette Banek
Author: Burton Marks
Designer: Patricia Jennings

First printing. Printed in Hong Kong.
Published simultaneously in Canada.

Time Life Inc. is a wholly owned subsidiary of THE TIME INC. BOOK COMPANY.

TIME-LIFE is a trademark of Time Warner Inc. U.S.A.

Time Life Inc. offers a wide range of fine publications, including home video products. For subscription information, call 1-800-621-7026, or write TIME-LIFE for CHILDREN, P.O. Box C-32068, Richmond, Virginia 23261-2068.

CONSULTANTS

Dr. Lewis P. Lipsitt, an internationally recognized specialist on childhood development, was the 1990 recipient of the Nicholas Hobbs Award for science in the service of children. He serves as science director for the American Psychological Association and is a professor of psychology and medical science at Brown University, where he is director of the Child Study Center.

Dr. Judith A. Schickedanz, an authority on the education of preschool children, is an associate professor of early childhood education at the Boston University School of Education, where she also directs the Early Childhood Learning Laboratory. Her published work includes *More Than the ABC's: Early Stages of Reading and Writing Development* as well as several textbooks and many scholarly papers.

Library of Congress Cataloging-in-Publication Data
The Bumbletown detectives.

 p. cm.–(Time-Life early learning program)
 Summary: Dame Edith and Sir Reginald decide to hire a detective to discover the thief at Mystery Manor, and the reader is encouraged to help with the clues.

 ISBN 0-8094-9270-9.—ISBN 0-8094-9271-7 (lib. bdg.)

 [1. Mystery and detective stories.] I. Time-Life for Children (Firm) II. Series.
PZ7.B9147 1991
[E]—dc20   91-8272
                                                CIP
                                                AC